This edition published by Parragon Books Ltd in 2016

Parragon Books Ltd
Chartist House
15–17 Trim Street
Bath BA1 1HA, UK
www.parragon.com

ISBN 978-1-4748-3287-8

Printed in China

Bath • New York • Cologne • Melbourne • Delhi
Hong Kong • Shenzhen • Singapore

Deep in the jungle, Bagheera the panther was out hunting. Suddenly, he heard a strange crying sound coming from the river.

He followed the sound and discovered a basket with a tiny baby boy inside.

"Why, it's a Man-cub!" he said. "This little chap needs food and a mother's care. Perhaps Mother Wolf will look after him."

Mother Wolf agreed to help. They named the Man-cub Mowgli and he grew up safe and happy in the jungle.

But everything changed when Mowgli was ten years old. Shere Khan, the man-eating tiger, heard about the Man-cub and came searching for him.

The wolves agreed that Bagheera should take the boy back to the Man-village where he would be safe.

So the next morning, Bagheera and Mowgli set off on their long journey. Mowgli was angry and upset. He didn't want to leave his home in the jungle.

When darkness fell, Bagheera and Mowgli climbed a tree and settled down to sleep on a branch. Nearby, hiding under some leaves, was Kaa, the python.

As soon as Bagheera was asleep, Kaa slithered towards the Man-cub. His shining eyes seemed to have a magic power and Mowgli quickly began to sink into a deep trance.

Slowly, Kaa started to wind himself around the boy, ready to swallow him up!

Suddenly, Bagheera woke up and sprang at Kaa. He struck the snake with his claws and sent him slithering away into the jungle.

At dawn, Mowgli was woken by a very loud noise. He looked down from the tree and saw Colonel Hathi and the Dawn Patrol marching along.

"Hup, two, three, four! Hup, two, three, four!" trumpeted the elephant.

Mowgli jumped down from the tree, got on all fours and joined the end of the parade behind a baby elephant. He had great fun, copying everything the little elephant did!

Eventually, Bagheera caught up with Mowgli and wanted to carry on towards the Man-village.

But Mowgli refused to go. He grabbed hold of a tree trunk and held on tightly.

Bagheera was very cross and ran off, leaving the Man-cub all alone.

It wasn’t long before Mowgli met a friendly bear called Baloo. He told Baloo how much he wanted to stay in the jungle.

“No problem!” Baloo said, “I’ll look after you!”

Baloo enjoyed teaching his new friend all about the ‘bare necessities of life’. Soon, Mowgli could fight like a bear, growl like a bear and even scratch like a bear!

Later that afternoon, Mowgli and Baloo waded into the river to keep cool. Mowgli sat on Baloo's tummy as they gently floated along. It was very peaceful and Baloo soon fell asleep.

But watching from some trees was a group of monkeys who were waiting to kidnap Mowgli.

The monkeys sprang out from their hiding place and grabbed the Man-cub.

Baloo woke with a jump but it was too late! The monkeys were already carrying Mowgli off to the ruined temple where they lived.

Luckily, Bagheera heard Mowgli's cries and rushed to the river to help. He found Baloo, who explained what had happened.

"We need a rescue plan," Bagheera said.

At the ruined temple, Louie, King of the Apes, was sitting on his throne waiting for the Man-cub to arrive.

"So, you're here at last!" Louie cried, as Mowgli was dropped beside him.

Louie offered to help Mowgli stay in the jungle. In return, he wanted to learn the secret of Man's red fire.

But before Mowgli could explain that he didn't know the secret, Louie declared that they would have a great feast in honour of their guest.

Baloo and Bagheera reached the temple just in time to see Louie leap from his throne and start to sing and dance in celebration of the Man-cub's arrival.

As Mowgli's feet began to tap to the music, he forgot his troubles and joined in the fun.

"Baloo," whispered Bagheera. "You distract the monkeys while I rescue Mowgli."

Baloo had an idea... He dressed in some coconut shells and leaves to make himself look like a lady ape. Then he waved at Louie.

The King thought the lady ape was very beautiful and rushed over to ask her to dance. He had no idea that it was really Baloo in disguise!

It wasn't long before Shere Khan spotted Mowgli in the distance. Emerging from the shadows, the tiger gave a loud roar.

He leaped at Mowgli, taking the Man-cub by surprise.

Mowgli refused to run from the tiger. Shere Khan counted to ten and then leaped at Mowgli, roaring, with all his claws out and his mouth wide open!

Baloo arrived in the nick of time and pulled Shere Khan's tail so hard, the tiger fell short of the Man-cub.

Shere Khan roared with rage as he dragged Baloo behind him, but the brave bear was determined not to let go.

Eventually, the furious tiger managed to flip Baloo over his head. The bear hit the ground with a mighty crash.

The vultures, Mowgli and Baloo all fought against Shere Khan. The tiger ran off when a lightning storm caused a tree to burst into flames and Mowgli tied a burning branch to his tail!

Baloo lay injured and still on the ground. Finally, he opened his eyes and lifted his head. Overjoyed, Mowgli ran and sprang into his friend's arms.

Baloo, Bagheera and Mowgli set off into the jungle once again, and at long last, they reached the Man-village.

Mowgli climbed a tree to get a good look at a girl he heard singing down by a watering hole. He couldn't take his eyes off her, to Bagheera's great delight. When the girl saw Mowgli, she smiled shyly at him.